# The Berenstain Bears
## and the
# SLUMBER PARTY

Sometimes little bears'
good behavior ends
when they pack their pajamas
and stay over with friends.

**A First Time Book**®

# The Berenstain Bears
### and the

## Stan & Jan Berenstain

Random House 🏠 New York

Copyright © 1990 by Berenstains, Inc. All rights reserved under International and Pan-American Copyright
Conventions. Published in the United States by Random House, Inc., New York, and simultaneously in
Canada by Random House of Canada Limited, Toronto.

*Library of Congress Cataloging-in-Publication Data:*
Berenstain, Stan. The Berenstain Bears and the slumber party / Stan & Jan Berenstain.   p.  cm.—
(First time books)   SUMMARY: Lizzy Bruin's slumber party becomes even wilder when Too-Tall Grizzly
and his friends decide to attend uninvited. ISBN 0-679-90419-0 (lib. bdg.)—ISBN 0-679-80419-6 (pbk.)
[1. Bears—Fiction.  2. Parties—Fiction.  3. Behavior—Fiction.]  I. Berenstain, Jan. II. Title.
III. Series: Berenstain, Stan. First time books.  PZ7.B4483Bfq  1990 [E]—dc20  89-35223  CIP  AC

Manufactured in the United States of America   10 9 8 7 6 5 4 3 2 1

One of the most interesting things about a telephone is that when it rings you don't know who's calling until you answer it. Sometimes when the phone rang in the Bears' tree house, it was for Papa. Papa Bear is a furniture maker, and customers often call about buying a table or chair.

Yes, I think I can handle that. How soon will you need it?

Sometimes it was Grizzly Gran calling Mama about getting together for a visit.

This weekend? That'll be fine, Gran.

When the call was for Brother Bear, it was usually Cousin Freddy with a question about homework.

The fifth problem? I got $6\frac{1}{2}$. What did you get?

When it was for Sister Bear, it was almost always her best friend, Lizzy Bruin.

For you, Sister.
It's Lizzy.

And Lizzy almost always had some big idea: a tea party for all their stuffed animals, going to the attic and dressing up in grownups' clothes, or organizing a sorority and using Farmer Ben's old chicken coop as a clubhouse— with permission, of course.

It's OK with me, but I think I should warn you...

PEE-YOO!

But today Lizzy was calling
with her best idea yet.
"A slumber party? Tonight
at your house? Great idea!"
said Sister.

"Just a few of my dearest friends," Lizzy continued. "You, of course, and Anna, Millie, and Queenie. Bring your sleeping bag—and would you bring your tape player? Anna and Millie are bringing tapes—and Queenie's going to teach us the latest dance steps."

"I don't know," Mama Bear
said later. "You've never slept
away from home before."

"Oh, but I have," protested
Sister. "At Grizzly Gramps and
Gran's—one time for a whole week!"

"That's different," said Mama.
"Gramps and Gran are family—
close family."

"The Bruins are neighbors," argued Sister. "*Close* neighbors. Oh please, Mama. It'll be such fun. I'm taking my player. Anna and Millie have great tapes—and Queenie is going to teach us the latest dance steps. Please, Mama."

"Oh, I suppose it's all right," sighed Mama. "Come on, let's start getting you organized for this slumber party."

"You know," she said as she checked out Sister's sleeping bag—it still had some leaves stuck to it from a family sleepout—"sleeping over at a friend's house is a kind of special privilege. And something that goes with privilege is responsibility. Do you know what those words mean?"

"Sure," said Sister. "Privilege means being allowed to do stuff, and responsibility means not messing up."

"Now, you remember what your mama told you about privilege and responsibility," said Papa Bear as Sister started off for Lizzy Bruin's.

"Oh, I will, Papa! I will!" she said.

But Sister wasn't very far along the road to Lizzy's before she began thinking about all the fun and excitement she was going to have at the party. It didn't take long for those thoughts to push Mama's advice about privilege and responsibility clear out of her head.

Another interesting thing about telephones is that they help news to travel fast—especially news about parties. Anna told her other friends about the slumber party, and they told their friends. Millie did the same. Pretty soon cubs from all over the neighborhood were calling Lizzy and asking if they could come to the party.

"Sure," she said. "But bring some popcorn or soda—we don't want to run out."

Too-Tall Grizzly didn't hear about
the party by phone. He heard about it
when he and his gang went to show
Queenie his new boom box.

"Hmm, a slumber party,"
he said to his pals. "Sounds
like fun."

"How are we gonna get invited to
a girls' party?" asked one of them.

"We're not gonna get invited,
stupid," said Too-Tall. "We're gonna
crash—boom box and all!"

Later, when the rest of the Bear family had settled down for a quiet evening at home, Mama Bear sighed and said, "I'm sure she'll be all right."

"Of course she will," said Papa Bear, looking up from a magazine.

"After all," Mama said, "Sister is a well-behaved little cub, and Mr. and Mrs. Bruin have a lovely, well-run home and are responsible, careful parents."

"No doubt about it," said Papa, going back to his reading.

There was only one problem:
*Mr. and Mrs. Bruin weren't home!*

They had gone out for the evening and had left Lizzy in the care of a teenage sitter who wasn't much older than some of Lizzy's guests. The Bruins hadn't planned on a slumber party when Lizzy had asked if a few friends could sleep over.

And they certainly hadn't planned on a rip-roaring, earsplitting, popcorn-throwing, soda-squirting party for half the cubs in the neighborhood. Because that's what was happening—with Sister right in the thick of it.

The only thing that wasn't happening at the slumber party was slumber.

Lizzy's sitter tried to keep things under control, but she couldn't even make herself heard over the noise. You never heard such a commotion! Some neighbors up the road had never heard such a commotion, either. They called the police.

The chief sent Officer Marguerite to investigate. She reached the Bruins' house at the same time Mr. and Mrs. Bruin were returning home.

Well, things calmed down pretty quickly after that. The party was canceled, parents were called, Lizzy was sent to bed—and an angry and disappointed Mama Bear came to take Sister home.

"I'm angry and disappointed," said Mama Bear as they walked home through the night. "After all the things I said about privilege and responsibility!"

Sister was grounded and sent to bed—*doubly* grounded, which meant she had to stay in her room for a day and in the house for a week.

"A pretty harsh punishment," commented Papa Bear a little later.

"Not harsh at all," said Mama. "You should have seen the Bruins' living room: popcorn stuck to everything, soda all over the place, lamps knocked over—an absolute disgrace! And after all I said about privilege and responsibility!"

"Sister does have to share the blame," said Papa. "But she didn't do it all by herself. It was one of those situations where one thing leads to another and things get out of control. But you know, my dear, privilege and responsibility aren't just for cubs. They're for parents, too."

"Cushions all strewn about—" said Mama.

"It's a privilege to have cubs—and with privilege goes responsibility," continued Papa. "So we're partly to blame too. When Lizzy invited Sister to the slumber party, it was our responsibility to call the Bruins. If we had, we'd have found out that they were going to be out for the evening, and the whole thing would have been nipped in the bud."

"Hmm," said Mama thoughtfully.

The next morning she canceled the grounding and took Sister over to the Bruins' to help clean up. Anna, Millie, and Queenie had come to help too.

"I know what!" said Lizzy,
as full of ideas as ever. "Let's
make this a clean-up party!"

"Let's not," said Sister. "And
if you don't mind, Liz, I don't
want to hear the word *party* again
for a long time."